Buster Changes His Luck

by Marc Brown

 LITTLE, BROWN AND COMPANY
New York ᨀ Boston

Little, Brown and Company, Time Warner Book Group
1271 Avenue of the Americas, New York, NY 10020 • www.lb-kids.com

First Edition: April 2006

Library of Congress Cataloging-in-Publication Data

Brown, Marc Tolon.
Buster changes his luck / by Marc Brown.—1st ed.   p. cm.—(Postcards from Buster)
"San Francisco—level 3."
Summary: Buster meets new friends in San Francisco's Chinatown who teach him about the Chinese New Year and good luck symbols in Chinese culture.
ISBN 0-316-15916-6 (hc) — ISBN 0-316-00129-5 (pb)
[1. Rabbits—Fiction. 2. Postcards—Fiction. 3. San Francisco (Calif.)—Fiction. 4. Chinatown (San Francisco, Calif.)—Fiction.] I. Title. II. Series: Brown, Marc Tolon. Postcards from Buster.
PZ7.B81618Bjbu 2006 [E]—dc22   2005002622

Printed in the United States of America • PHX • 10 9 8 7 6 5 4 3 2 1

All photos, except page 3, from the *Postcards from Buster* television series courtesy of WGBH Boston and Cookie Jar Entertainment Inc. in association with Marc Brown Studios.

Do you know what these words MEAN?

ancestors (AN-ses-ters): relatives from long ago

bamboo (bam-BOO): a tropical plant with a long hollow stem

culture: the way in which a certain group of people lives

fulfillment: the act of making something happen

longevity (lon-JEH-vuh-tee): how long a person lives

San Francisco (SAN frun-SIS-ko): a large city in California

respect: to treat with consideration

scroll: a piece of paper rolled up in a fancy way

San Francisco

- The city of San Francisco is built on 43 hills.

- The Golden Gate Bridge is actually orange, but when the sun shines it glows and looks golden.

- San Francisco's nickname is the City by the Bay.

"Buster, aren't you taking any snacks on this trip?" asked Arthur.

Buster shook his head. "No time to pack them. I'll pick up something when we get to San Francisco."

Buster was very hungry
when the plane finally landed.

He tried to get some food
from a vending machine.
It didn't work.

Then he bought some doughnuts,
but he left them in the taxi.

Dear Arthur,

Getting snacks
out here
is harder
than I expected.

But my stomach
and I are
not giving up yet!

Buster

Buster and Mora went looking
for more doughnuts in Chinatown.

They approached a vegetable stand
with taro root and Chinese cabbage.

"These look good," said Buster,
"but I'm not giving up on doughnuts yet."

"Oh, look!" said Mora.
"A dim sum place.
It's a restaurant where you can try
all kinds of food."

"I wonder if they have doughnuts,"
said Buster.
"Hmmm . . . the menu is in Chinese."

Buster asked two girls
standing nearby for help.

"Hi, I'm Buster."

"I'm Kary," said one girl.

"I'm Hayley," said the other.

Dear Francine,

I met two girls who tried to order Chinese doughnuts for me.

But the restaurant was out of them.

My snack curse lives on!

Buster

Buster noticed that the girls were carrying tangerines.

"They mean good luck for the new year," said Kary.

"But New Year's was almost a month ago," said Buster.

"This is the Chinese New Year," Kary explained.
"It uses a different calendar based on the moon."

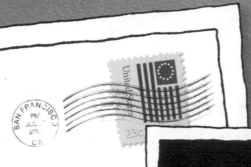

Alan "The Brai...
22 Oak Street
Elwood City,

"Are these scrolls for sale?"
asked Buster.

"Yes," said Kary. She picked one up.
"This means good luck.
You hang it upside down.
That way the luck will pour down
on your head."

Dear Mom,

I will soon be covered with good luck.

Don't worry, it won't mess up my clothes.

Buster

In another part of the market, Buster met Hayley's and Kary's moms.

Kary's mom was still looking for bamboo. "It means good luck and longevity," she said, "because bamboo is very strong."

"Then let's find it," said Buster. "I need all the luck I can get."

Dear Binky,

For the Chinese New Year
you wear new clothes
to disguise yourself
so that bad spirits
won't find you.

Do you think that would
work on Mr. Ratburn?

Buster

Binky B
10 Pine
Elwoo

Buster found a green vest
with dragons on it.

"Dragons bring luck," said Kary.

"They scare away evil spirits,"
her mother added.

"I'll take it!" said Buster.

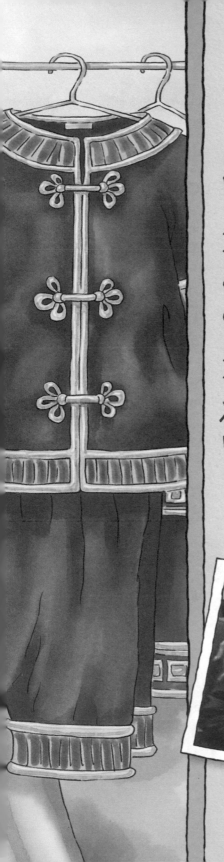

Dear Muffy,

I'm learning a lot
about fashion
on this trip.

I'd be glad to give
you some pointers
when I get back.

Buster

In a stationery store,
Buster found all kinds of paper goods.

"There's the red stuff," said Buster,
"and then there's the other red stuff."

"Red is a color that brings good luck,"
said Mora.

"Oh," said Buster.
"Then I definitely should get some."

ELIZA

"Hey, Mom," said Kary, "can Buster eat Chinese New Year dinner with us?"

"Sure," said her mother.

"Thank you," said Buster. "I'll make sure to bring as much good luck as I can."

The next day Buster was late getting ready because his clock had stopped.

Then he couldn't get the elevator to work.

And he bumped into someone who spilled soda on his clothes.

SORRY!
REPAIRS
IN
PROGRESS

Dear Francine,

I ate a whole bag
of tangerines
last night.

I slept next to
some bamboo.
I'm even
wearing dragons.

Can you believe
I'm still having
such terrible luck?

Buster

When Buster reached Kary's house,
he was feeling as unlucky as ever.

"Maybe this candy will help," said Kary.
"You should always start the new year
with something sweet."

"I haven't had anything sweet today,"
said Buster. "Maybe that's my problem."

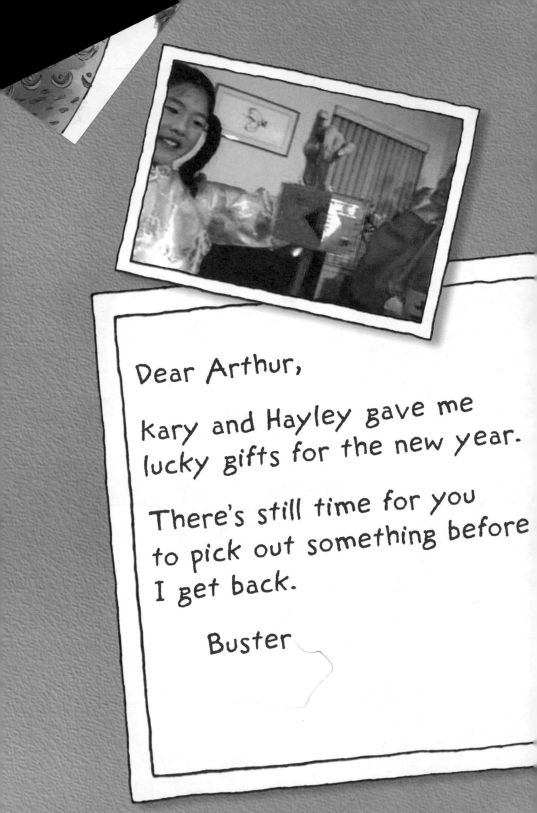

Dear Arthur,

Kary and Hayley gave me lucky gifts for the new year.

There's still time for you to pick out something before I get back.

Buster

Arthur Read
100 Main Street
Elwood City,

"Hey, guys, it's dinnertime,"
said Kary's mom.

"Before we eat," said Kary,
"we show respect
to the god of heaven, our ancestors,
and the god of our home."

"How do you show respect?"
Buster asked.

"Like this," said Kary.
"You put your hands like a fist
and bow three times."

"This all looks so good," said Buster. "What are the different dishes?"

"The one next to me means long life." said Kary.

"And this second dish," said Hayley, "means fulfillment of happiness and wealth."

Binky Barnes
10 Pine ~~~~ Road
Elwood

"So is this dinner the last big celebration for the new year?" Buster asked.

"Well," said Kary, "there's also a Chinese New Year's parade."

"It may be the largest celebration of Chinese culture in the whole country," said Kary's mom.

Dear D.W.,

I am going to watch a big parade tomorrow.

I have so much good luck now that I'm sure I will like it.

Buster

Dear Arthur,

The Chinese New Year parade included a dancing imp and gold monkeys, and Kary dressed as a slice of pizza.

Did you know there is Chinese pizza?

I didn't.

Buster

At last Buster saw the dragons.

The biggest one was orange and green.

"Just listen to those firecrackers,"
said Mora. "They have to be
loud enough to scare off
all the bad spirits for a whole year."

"Then keep them coming," said Buster.
"Woo-hoo! Happy New Year!"

Dear Kary and Hayley,

Remember how I had bad
luck getting snacks?
I've been thinking . . .

That led to my
meeting you.
So it turned out to be
the very best luck of all.

Buster

DISCARD HFLOX + BROWN